T0197541

Annie Lilypod
in the
Time Zone

CAT
RAT
MAT

Marie Angel Bethel

This is an unforgettable story of a beautiful young girl named Annie Lilypod—a teenage girl who came from a loving family. Her parents were a biracial couple name Henry and Hermione Lilypod. Her mother was black, and her father was white. They were a professional couple, in which the father was a doctor and the mother a registered nurse. They owned a dress shop and were very active members in the community of the town of Maha. They had one child, a lovely daughter named Annie, and they loved her very much. Annie was sent to the most expensive private school in the city.

Everyone in the town of Maha adored them because they were kind to the citizens. Moreover, they were a very hardworking business couple. They also donated money, clothing, and food to the poor in their district.

Their daughter, Annie, loved the outdoors and enjoyed being in their beautiful flower and vegetable gardens. She adored helping the caretaker to water the gardens, because she loved the smell of sweet daffodils and roses and also admired the green vegetables that were growing in the garden. She also enjoyed looking at the birds on the trees and the cows grazing in the meadow. She spent most of her time under an oak tree, reading a book or singing or sometimes looking at the different colors of birds sitting on the trees.

Then one day, she was in the garden and saw an amazing bunch of little blue flowers shaped like a bell growing on a vine. Finally, she thought it was quite interesting and decided to investigate. However, while picking the flowers, she observed a little doorknob hidden behind these beautiful blue flowers. Then Annie opened the door and went into a strange flower garden that had the most beautiful flowers she had ever seen. However, she thought it was a very unusual place, but continued to acquire it.

Then she saw a red bird sitting on the tree. It was singing beautifully, and it was quite amazing. On the other hand, there came two rabbits, all dressed up in clothes like human beings, that could talk. She was terrified, but the rabbits told her not to be afraid, as they would not hurt her.

One of the rabbits said, "This is a very friendly, loving place, and everyone are very happy and kind."

She then introduced herself to the rabbit, "My name is Annie Lilypod, and I am lost and would like to go back home."

The rabbit said, "I do not know how to get you back home. Do you remember the entrance you came from?"

She pointed over there that there was a door in that area. They looked everywhere in the garden, but did not find the door. She sat down on the grass and cried. All the other animals came out and comforted her, reassuring her that they would continue to search for that invisible door decorated with the blue bellflowers, which would take Annie back to her home. They invited her to their world and tried their best to make her comfortable at all times.

But as the days passed by, Annie was always thinking about her parents and friends; furthermore, she hoped to return home soon. Meanwhile, her parents were looking for her and thought maybe someone had kidnapped her.

The search continued for many years, but they never found her. They knew that the gardener said that she was at a fence, picking those blue flowers. Then all of a sudden, he did not see her anymore and thought maybe she had left and was in the house. The town of Maha was grief-stricken and searched for her for several years, but Annie was never found. They all thought she was kidnapped and maybe she was dead.

It was a difficult time for the parents to lose their only beautiful child, who was fifteen years old. The people in the town were heartbroken and mourned and prayed for her all the time.

Many years had passed by, but she was not found. And then her parents, grief-stricken, sold the house and the store because it was too painful to live there anymore. They bought a new home in another part of the village. Her parents believed that she was dead and was with the Heavenly Father, resting peacefully.

Later on, as the years went by, her father died from natural illness. Her mother was grief-stricken, and her mother sold the house and opened a children's home that would give her mother fresh courage and a new lifestyle. Her mother helped many children that didn't have a home. This project had given her mother comfort and joy, but she never forgot her beautiful Annie, and she continued to live a quiet lifestyle.

Annie met a lot of friends, but they were all animals. She decided to just relax and do whatever she could do instead of crying and worrying about her parents and best friends. As a very educated young girl, she decided to teach the animals and was quite amazed that they sat down on the grass and listened to her.

As time went by, she felt more relaxed but hoped to return home one day. Annie was always thinking about her parents and friends that she had left behind. Regarding that she came here by mistake, hopefully, one day she would return home to her families and friends.

The animals acted just like humans and took good care of her. They made clothing, shoes, bags, and hats for her. They had given her a house and everything she needed, and they loved her. The animals were magical beings, which talked and acted just like human beings.

Their world was named Animas, a magical world. Annie fed all the large animals that lived on the meadows. Their food came from the trees, and it was a beautiful, quiet place—no one fought, insulted, and cursed, and no awful languages. They all respected each other and made Annie their queen and adored her. They had given her a servant and did everything for her. It was not the normal meal that she was accustomed to, but it was more vegetables. Even their cakes and treats were all made of vegetables. They really lived very well and were indeed healthy. All their food came from the land. They adored everything that was being grown on the land. She thought it was the most quiet and happy-go-lucky place that anyone could live in.

Annie missed her parents terribly, but realized that this was her new home, until a miracle happened that she could return to her home one day. She prayed all the time that she would find a way to go home, because she missed her parents, families, and friends terribly. She also accepted that this was her new home and made it the best she could. However, feeding the big animals, it gave her fresh courage that it was not so bad.

She wondered, *Since they can talk, why not make a school and teach them the things I knew?* This was always her dream—to be a teacher. This helped Annie quite a bit, and every day, she prayed to find that invisible door that led her into this world. She knew that day would come, but she was happy to experience this quite magical, talking, animal world that they lived in with peace and harmony.

She hoped that her world, the Earth, could have that kind of peace and tranquility. They had no television, but they did magical things to make her laugh, and sometimes, she spent the day under a large oak tree and looked at the blue sea and the wonderful trees and flowers that surrounded the area. It was a marvelous, quiet, magical place, and everyone loved each other, no fights or bad words. It seemed everyone really adored and respected each other. She wished, in her heart, the world she came from would be like this world—a world with love and magic.

They made her clothing magically, and they asked her everyday what kind of dinner or breakfast she would like to eat. On this lovely sunny day, she said, "I will love a delicious bowl of split peas soup, salad, a vegetarian burger, and apple pie with vanilla ice cream." There it was before her on the table. She knew that they were animals, so she never asked for meat or fish dishes. She knew it would be an insult and very disrespectful, and she would not do that.

The animals of this strange world were so kind and helpful to her. When they had taken her to their house, they had told her to think about the home she left behind, and they magically built the same model of the home she left. She described all the furniture, and her house was decorated exactly as she wanted it to be, with all the comforts she needed.

They had given her servants, who wore clothing and shoes just like humans, but their faces were like a pig, dog, mouse, chicken, rabbit, etc. They spoke nicely and had done everything for her. They took care of her, just as her servant had done in her homeland.

She played the piano and sang songs. One older female animal was very close to her and helped her a lot. They held a birthday party for her when she was eighteen years old, and she honored what they had done for her. It was just like her home. They made a big cake from vegetables, and her best animal friends came to the party. Annie was given all the traditional takings of a birthday party, and was quite a happy girl.

Even with all the wonderful surroundings she had, she still missed her home and would always think about her parents and friends. She had never given up hope that she would return home to her parents one day. Now she was eighteen years old, and she prayed to go back home every night. Although the animals had given her a wonderful birthday party, she still wanted to go home, because she realized, "I am getting older and my parents are older and might die."

Everyday her animal friends kept on looking for that magical door, but never found it. Until one day, when Annie went into the garden, the two rabbits–her best friends–were sitting on the grass between some trees, and she was just walking around the garden and noticed the same beautiful little blue bellflowers growing on a long vine. She was amazed and thought, *These were the same flowers that I touched and my hands were on a doorknob.*

She decided to pick the blue flowers, and she touched a doorknob. The door opened and she walked in. Regrettably, it was not her world, but a medieval world. She was quite afraid, standing in a rocky area. Unfortunately, she happened to enter a time zone of the medieval world. She stood quite afraid, watching the trees, and saw a man on a horse coming toward her. As he came closer to her, she realized that he was a soldier. He came off his horse, tied it to a tree, and came toward her.

He said, "Hello, Miss, are you alone in this part of the forest?"

She was confused and amazed that this was a real human being. She said, "My name is Annie Lilypod, and I am lost."

He said, "My name is Captain Murphy, Prince of Edge Town, pleased to meet you, and you need to come with me because it is not safe here when the sun goes down."

She said, "I will like to say goodbye to my friends, because they took good care of me and comforted me."

He said, "All right."

But they could not find the entrance to that animal world. She was very sad, remembering that she always told them thank you, in case one day, an unexpected return to her world would happen, just as she came to this medieval world. She knew when the animal people, her friends, did not see her, they would realize that she had found the door and went back home.

Annie found a door, but unfortunately, it was to the medieval world. Captain Murphy put her on his horse and took her to his city. She was a bit scared, but felt great that she was in the company of a human being again. They rode for many miles to his home, and he took her into the palace.

He called his mother and father to greet her. They were happy to meet her, because Annie was so beautiful, with dark brown curly hair and hazel eyes. His parents adored her immediately. She was given an elegant bedroom and servants.

Annie was quite surprised, but was very happy that she was living among human beings again. But sometimes, she would still think about her magical animal friends. The king and the queen adored her and wanted their son to marry her. She told them all about the mysteries of her life, the animal people, her parents, and her hopes of seeing them one day. At that moment, she was quite happy and very comfortable. This was in another dimension, which she only read about this type of lifestyles.

As time passed by, the prince wanted to marry her, and his parents agreed. They had a wonderful wedding, and all the people of Edge Town came to celebrate. They adored Annie Lilypod—her beauty was astonishing. It was a town that came together to celebrate with the king and queen. On that special day, she was married and wore a beautiful white lace gown and a lovely diamond crown. The people were gathered outside to see them and cheered in their happy moment. She always thought about her parents, and she wished that they were there. But she hoped to get back to her world with her prince by her side.

She lived very happy but has never forgotten her parents. She loved playing the piano and taking long walks in the garden. As the months passed by, she had a baby boy, and she was so happy. She said, "I wish my parents can see him." She had difficult times because of her past life, but a lot of better moments. However, regardless of how happy she was, she never forgot her parents and friends and the animal world she left behind. She continued praying and hoping to meet her family again.

She had a beautiful son, but never allowed the maids to take her son into the garden. She told them to watch him while he played in the courtyard. She was afraid that it might happen to her son. The servants were ordered to constantly watch him as he played. As years passed by, her father died, but her mother moved on to a new home. Annie had a son and a daughter; but again, she was very cautious of the same garden situation, and kept them away from the garden.

Many years had gone by, and the prince's father and mother had died from natural causes. Her husband became king, and she was queen. The people adored them, but she has never forgotten her parents. She wondered, *Are they alive still or maybe they died?* But she hoped to go back to her world one day.

One day, she and the king went walking in the garden with their children. She noticed the little blue bellflowers. The prince he knew about Annie's history in the garden.

She said, "I am sure that there is a door there, and it might be my world that I came from."

The king said, "Do not touch the vine, it might be magical, and we might end up in another world."

His idea was to mark the area by putting a ribbon on the doorknob, so in case they opened it, they might be able to get back home. They did put the ribbon and other ornaments to mark the spot, plus a guard stood between the doorways. They left the children with the nanny, and they went through the door. From the minute they came through the door, she recognized, "This is my world."

"This is exactly where I was at fifteen years old." She saw the house, and a lot of vines grew upon the house, and it seemed no one was there. The king left his sword and a guard standing between the doorway. They went into the house, but no one was there. It seemed as though no one was in the house for many years. They went to the neighbor next door, and the neighbor told her what had happened to her parents, that her father died from natural causes, and the neighbor also told her where her mother was living.

They went and looked for her mother who was quite older, because Annie was in her late forties. Annie was so happy to see her mom, who had retired from nursing many years ago, and she told her mother to come and live with her and meet her grandchildren, and that now she is Queen Annie Murphy Lilypod, and the people love her. Her mother decided to go with them and gave her house to her wonderful servants and shared other possessions with the poor in the village of Maha.

They returned to the medieval world, and her mother had lived in the palace with her. They never told anyone about the door to another world, and they did not want to go back to their world. That world Annie and her mom left was a very noisy and busy world. She adored the people around her and the world she was in. The people liked her and no one knew about the world she left behind or the door in the garden that led to another world. The king had blocked that part of the garden so his children, or no one, could go to the other side of another world. They may not be as lucky as Annie Lilypod and might get killed. They never talked about it or told anyone about it. They were happy and contented, and her mom lived for a few more years and died in this medieval world. No one knew anything about their lives from a busy, corrupted world.

This story of Annie Lilypod is based on how one left their country and came to another country, and how some people never returned home and died in that new country. Your country might be very quiet, then you arrived in this new world that is like in another dimension.

Life is quite different—it might have a faster pace, might be very noisy, might be equipped with electrical appliances that you are not used to, and you have to adjust from walking to taking a bus, train, or even learn to drive a car. It is all new and can be a frightening experience.

It happened to me coming to another country—Canada and United Kingdom—many, many years ago. Experiencing snow is a big one, and even having your own telephone and television is another big one. It can be frightening—the big roads, fast cars, huge buildings, brighter lights, and very busy people of many races who are not saying anything to one another, not even good day. There were no donkey carts, no rivers next to the town to swim in, no one with a van calling out to get your ice, no one sharpening knife and scissors or soldering cooking enamel pots and pans when there are holes or damages, no fruit trees, no children playing in the yard, spinning tops, flying kites, or jumping over ropes. Nothing like that.

Children in a new world are equipped with electronic things, such as computers, phones, calculators, etc. Technicolor televisions and water taps are in their house, a better life setting. I still miss the old days when everyone respected each other, when there were a lot of big mamas who took care of children when their parents were working. Big mama will spank you if they catch you doing the wrong things. You dare not tell your parents; otherwise, you might receive a spanking for bad behavior. When your parents say, "Jump," you say, "How high." You eat whatever is in front of you without complaints—a rule of thumb. It takes a village to raise a child, and so were the good days. Respect, respect, and care for and help each other–those were the good days. Now we are on the fast track. Fast food in a microwave, not on the stove, no coal pots, or dirt fire stoves. Mostly, no one has the time to greet each other. How I missed the good old days. Sometimes, I want to be like Annie Lilypod in the time zone.

Moreover, everybody is very busy going about their businesses, no one cares to say good day or even say hello. This time zone is reality, just like Annie had experienced. It must have been a very difficult time. She had to adjust to the strange situations, just like I and others had to. Sometimes, we would like to go back to our world, but we could not because of our situations. Sometimes, we would love the new world and would hope for the best. We had to adjust to various things. Our experience of the new world was difficult, but we tried our best to continue. Sometimes, we wondered what we could do if we went back to our world. Is there anybody around? Many people have died, and the new ones, we do not know them.

Sometimes, our own families would change, and we would not know their siblings or new neighbors. It makes it very difficult. We are just like Annie Lilypod in the time zone. We are in a new place and have to adjust to the things we are not used to, such as experiencing the trains, the fast cars, the busy wide roads, extremely bright lights, and loud music.

Everyone is hustling to go about their business. No one has the time to say hello or good day. We are not sure about anything, but we press forward, and this is exactly what happened to Annie. She did go back, but met a prince who became a king, and she took her mother to live with her. And she lived happily ever after. Sometimes, we are better in the time zone.

To order additional copies of this book, contact:
Xlibris
844-714-8691
www.Xlibris.com
Orders@Xlibris.com

ISBN: Softcover   978-1-6698-4870-7
       Hardcover   978-1-6698-4871-4
       EBook   978-1-6698-4869-1

Print information available on the last page

Rev. date: 11/30/2022

Printed in the United States
by Baker & Taylor Publisher Services